This book belongs to

_____

Janet Hissey
Jolly Snow

SCRIBBLERS

IT was cold and grey outside. Jolly Tall, the giraffe, was gazing out of the window.

'Are you waiting for something?' asked Rabbit.

'I'm waiting for it to snow,' said Jolly. 'I've never seen snow.'

'I know where there's some,' said Little Bear.

HE hurried away and returned with a large glass bubble. Inside, a little house and a tree were covered in tiny snowflakes. Jolly stared at the snow.

'It's very pretty,' he said. 'What can you do with it?'

'You can make snowballs,' said Little Bear.

'And slide on it,' said Zebra.

'Or jump in it,' said Rabbit, 'and make footprints.'

'There doesn't look enough of it for that,' said Jolly.

HOLDING the glass bubble tightly, Little Bear jumped up and down. The snowflakes rushed around inside the glass.

'Look at it now!' he cried.

'There's not enough to make a snowball,' said Jolly.

'And you can't get it out,' grumbled Duck.

'I know where there's lots of snow,' said Zebra.

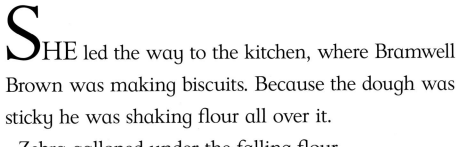

SHE led the way to the kitchen, where Bramwell
Brown was making biscuits. Because the dough was
sticky he was shaking flour all over it.

Zebra galloped under the falling flour.

'Whoopee!' she cried. 'A snowstorm!'

In no time at all, her black stripes
had almost disappeared.

RABBIT tried to pick up a pawful of flour.

'It doesn't stick together,' he said. 'You can't make snowballs.'

'The dough balls are fun, though,' said Little Bear. He threw one at Rabbit and it stuck to his bottom.

'Now you have two tails,' laughed Little Bear.

Zebra was jumping up and down. 'The flour-snow doesn't come off,' she said.

'Oh dear,' said Bramwell, 'you need a bath!'

T HEY filled a bowl with soapy water and the snowy
Zebra climbed in. She splashed and sploshed and bubbles
went everywhere.

'Snow-bubbles!' cried Little Bear, popping them with his
paws. 'Your bath is full of them.'

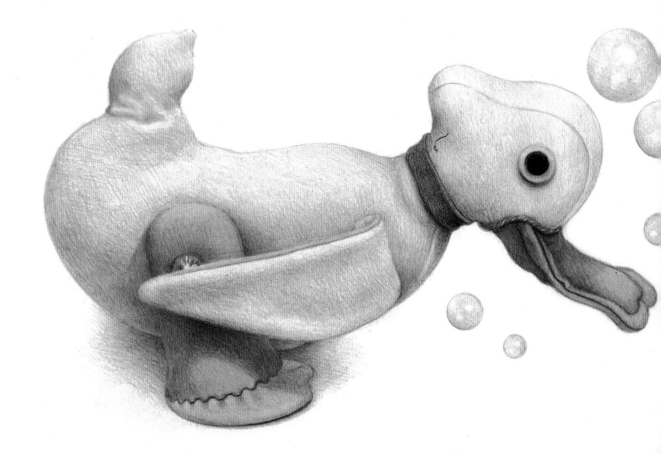

THEY rubbed and scrubbed until Zebra was stripy
again. Then they wrapped her in a warm towel.
  'Now we can play with the snow-bubbles,' said
Little Bear.

HE rushed over to Zebra's bath and stared.

'Where have all the bubbles gone?' he cried. 'I wanted them for Jolly.'

'Bubbles never last,' said Duck, 'and they make very sloppy snow. Let's ask Old Bear how we can make snow.'

OLD Bear was making paper decorations. He'd made paper stars, paper bells and paper lanterns. He'd even made paper snowflakes.

'You can't really play with these,' said Little Bear, trying to slide on one.

'That's because they are just for looking at,' said Old Bear.

'We want some snow for Jolly,' explained Rabbit, 'snow you *can* play with.'

'WHAT about these?' said Old Bear, scattering a blizzard of paper pieces in the air.

'They're lovely,' said Rabbit.

'And they're slippery!' said Little Bear as he ran at them, sat down and skidded across the room.

'We need a sledge now,' said Rabbit, 'or you'll wear out your trousers.'

THEY found a cardboard box and cut away the sides. Rabbit tied a string to the front to pull it along.

'It works,' cried Little Bear.

'If we had a slope to go down, it would be even better,' said Rabbit.

Bramwell found a big white sheet.

'Here's your slope,' he said. 'We'll hold it up and you can slide down!'

Little Bear and Rabbit climbed onto the sledge.

' Ready,

Steady,

GO!'

they called.

B<small>RAMWELL</small> and Jolly lifted the sheet.
The sledge whizzed down the slope, across the
room and into the wall on the other side.

'WE need a softer landing,' said Rabbit, fluffing up his flattened fur.

They piled cushions against the wall and pulled the sledge back on the sheet.

'One,
        Two,
                Three,
                        GO!'

they called to Jolly.

U P went the sheet, down went the toys, straight into the heap of cushions.

As they landed, clouds of feathers puffed out of a little hole in a cushion.

'FEATHER-snow!' cried Little Bear, jumping on the cushion to make more feathers come out.

Soon all the toys were playing with the feathers. They rolled in them and jumped in them and piled them in heaps.

'Is this like real snow?' asked Jolly.

'It's better,' laughed Little Bear. 'It doesn't melt or make you cold. Let's put some round the windows.'

HE began to pile feathers in each corner of the window.

'Someone's already done this one,' he called.

The window was all white but it was on the outside!

'It isn't feathers,' cried Little Bear. 'Look, Jolly, it's real snow!'

The toys stared out of the window.

'Now we can play outside,' said Zebra.

BUT just then Bramwell arrived with a plate of his special snowflake biscuits.

'I think you all need some of *my* snow first,' he laughed.

Jolly thought about the flour-snow and the paper-snow, the feather-snow and the bubble-snow. Then he looked at the real snow floating down outside.

'I like all kinds of snow,' he announced. 'But,' he added, as he munched a snowflake biscuit, 'Bramwell's snow is probably the snow I like best!'

For Ralph

SALARIYA

www.salariya.com

This edition published in Great Britain in MMXIII by Scribblers, a division of Book House,
an imprint of The Salariya Book Company Ltd
25 Marlborough Place,
Brighton BN1 1UB

www.scribblersbooks.com
www.janehissey.co.uk

First published in Great Britain in MCMXCI by Hutchinson Children's Books

HB ISBN-13: 978-1-908973-02-3
PB ISBN-13: 978-1-908973-70-2

1 3 5 7 9 8 6 4 2

A CIP catalogue record for this book is available from the British Library.

Printed and bound in China
Printed on paper from sustainable sources

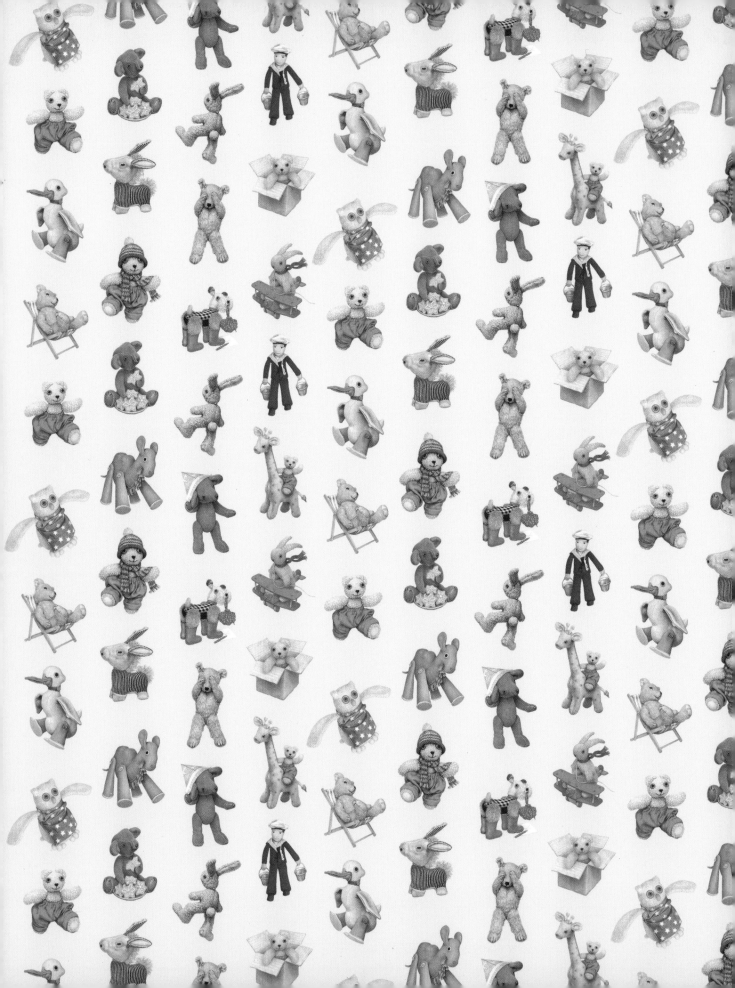